KIKA Superwitch

Bruño

Título original: *Lilli the Witch – Trouble at School*

Textos ingleses: Ellen Butzko
Ilustraciones: Birgit Rieger

Este libro se ha negociado a través de Ute Körner Literary Agent, S. L.

Juan Ignacio Luca de Tena, 15; 28027 Madrid

www.brunolibros.es

Dirección del Proyecto Editorial: Trini Marull
Dirección Editorial: Isabel Carril
Edición: Cristina González
Revisión y adaptación de textos ingleses: John Liddy y Sixto J. Cámara
Traducción de textos alemanes: Alberto Simal
Diseño de cubierta: Miguel Ángel Parreño
Preimpresión: Mar Morales

ISBN: 978-84-216-9554-8
Depósito legal: M-15974-2011

Printed in Spain

KNISTER

KIKA Superwitch

Trouble at School

Bruño

7.ª edición

KNISTER

Vive en Alemania. Escribe libros y también es músico. Chalado, gracioso y divertido... ¡siempre! Su color favorito: el del arco iris. Su comida favorita: los espaguetis, a cualquier hora del día. Su mayor hobby: tocar en una banda de rock. Su signo del zodiaco: rana.

Ellen Butzko

Nació en 1963 y es profesora de inglés en un colegio de Alemania. Forma parte de un grupo de trabajo de didáctica en la escuela, y ha preparado este libro de Kika en inglés para ti.

Birgit Rieger

Vive y trabaja en Berlín. Es diseñadora gráfica independiente, y le encanta ilustrar libros para niños y jóvenes.

John Liddy y Sixto J. Cámara

Los dos son profesores de inglés en España. John es, además, *teacher librarian,* y Sixto también es coordinador del proyecto bilingüe inglés-español en el colegio público Rufino Blanco de Madrid.

Nota para los padres
y profesores → pág. 84
Trucos de lectura
ultrasecretos
de Kika → pág. 88

Magic words

book of witchcraft: libro de brujería
broom: escoba
magic: magia, mágico
magic book: libro de magia
magic broom: escoba mágica
magic spell: hechizo mágico
magic trick: truco de magia
secret: secreto
secret book: libro secreto
secret magic: magia secreta
secret witch: bruja secreta
spell: hechizo
Superwitch: Superbruja
trick: truco
trick of witchcraft: truco de brujería
witch: bruja
witchcraft: brujería

This is Kika.
She's your age
and looks like
a normal child.
She *is* a normal
child, but . . .
not really. Kika has a book.
This is *not* a normal book:
it's a book of witchcraft.
One morning Kika looks under her bed –
and surprise, surprise:
there it is, the book of witchcraft!
Kika has no idea who put it there.
But she knows that
the book is full of real magic
and wild tricks.
Kika can do some of these tricks.
But careful!

looks like: parece
wild tricks: trucos alucinantes
careful: cuidado

If *you* do these tricks,
it can be very dangerous:
one wrong word and –
a magic broom turns into a skateboard,
a teacher turns into a penguin,
ice-cream turns into a carrot.
That's why nobody knows
that Kika has this book.
That's why nobody knows
that she's a secret witch.
And that's why Dani doesn't know
that she can do magic tricks.
Who's Dani?
He's Kika's little brother.
Dani asks lots of questions.
Little brothers can really
get on your nerves!
But Kika loves her
little brother very much . . .
Let's start with our story then.

dangerous: peligroso
skateboard: monopatín
carrot: zanahoria
can get on your nerves: poner de los nervios
our: nuestra

Chapter 1

"Kika, Kika, I have to tell you something!"
Oh no, it's Dani!
He's getting on Kika's nerves again.
It's Tuesday afternoon.
School is over.
Dani was there with his mother today.
He was there to register
for the first school year.

is over: ha acabado
to register: matricularse

Dani is so happy to go to school.
He wants to tell Kika how good
his first day was at school.
"Kika, Kika, where are you?
I want to tell you something."
Kika wants to be alone.
She's under her bed
but Dani finds her there.
"Kika, Kika, I was at school today
for an interview with the headmaster,"
Dani says.
"Can you believe it, Kika?
He asked me two questions.
He asked me where's left?
and where's right?
and – of course I knew the answer!"
Kika says: "Of course you know

alone: sola
headmaster: director
Can you believe it?: ¿Puedes creértelo?
of course I knew: por supuesto que sabía

the answer to these two questions!"
Dani is very proud. He says:
"Well, . . . just one little mistake . . ."
Kika answers: "Wonderful,
only one mistake with left and right.
That's clever!"
Kika's mum stands in the door now.
Kika winks at her.
Dani says: "Well, I'm a big pupil now."
"Just you wait!" mother says.
"School can be hard."
"Not so fast!" Kika says.
"School is not what you think."
"Wait and see!" Dani says.
"School will be super!"

proud: orgulloso
That's clever: ¡Qué listo!
winks: guiña un ojo
pupil: estudiante, alumno
Just you wait!: ¡Alto ahí!
Not so fast!: ¡No tan rápido!
Wait and see!: ¡Ya veréis!
will be: será

Mother goes back
into the living-room. Dani can't leave
Kika alone. He wants to know
more about school.
"What about you? Nice day at school?"
Dani is talking like a really big pupil now.
Kika answers: "Just a normal day."
Dani wants to know:
"Well, what's normal for you?"
Kika is fed up: "Just normal,
I did some reading and writing and . . ."
but then Kika remembers:
". . . but tomorrow something special
is going to happen.
An inspector is going to come
to our school tomorrow.

fed up: molesta
remembers: se acuerda
is going to happen: va a pasar

He's going to sit in our class
and watch our teacher."
Dani doesn't understand.
"And why?"
Kika tells him: "He wants to check
on Ms Howard, our teacher."
Now, Dani understands:
"Ah, so is this inspector like
a policeman for teachers?"
"Yes, something like that,"
Kika answers. "He checks on teachers.
He wants to see
that they do a good job.

to check on: supervisar

And tomorrow he's going
to check on Ms Howard."
Now Dani really understands
everything: "Oh, he's
like a sheriff then.
He walks through town.
And when he sees a bad man –
BANG, BANG, BANG!"
"No, Dani, *that* is not going to happen
tomorrow," Kika laughs. "I don't think
he has a revolver!
He just wants to see that we learn
the right things from Ms Howard.
Ms Howard says we must be
very nice tomorrow and very polite."
"Polite??? What's that?" Dani asks.
"You're polite, for example,
if you don't forget to say PLEASE.

town: ciudad
learn: aprendemos
forget: olvidas

Or if you say ›sir‹, not ›uncle‹
to a man that you don't know.
Or . . ."
"Or if I give my seat on the bus
to mummy's friend
so she can sit down.
Or if somebody farts
and it stinks like in the zoo
and I think I'm going to die
but I'm polite and I just say:
›Don't worry, I can't smell a thing!‹"
Kika giggles: "Yes, you're right,
that's polite. You are a clever boy!
And now you can be a clever pupil
and leave me alone
so I can do my homework."

sir: señor
seat: asiento
farts: se tira un pedo
stinks: apesta
a thing: nada
giggles: se ríe
leave me alone: déjame sola

Dani is happy now.
He takes one of Kika's comics
and goes out of the room.
Kika is alone.
She closes the door.
Then she gets a chair . . .
Nobody can come in now.

Why does she do that?
<u>That's simple</u>:
Kika must be alone because
she wants to do secret magic.
She has a brilliant idea.
An idea for tomorrow . . .

<u>That's simple</u>: Muy sencillo

Chapter 2

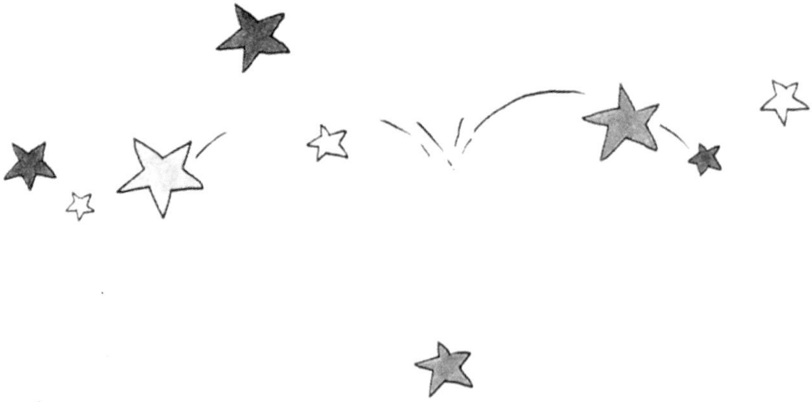

Kika finds her magic book of witchcraft under her bed. Then she gets a pencil and a piece of paper.
Now she can write down her ideas.

"Let's see," Kika says.
She goes through her magic book.
All these wonderful magic tricks!
The book is in alphabetical order.
Under B she finds
something about BROOMS,

goes through: hojea

under F she finds
something about FIREWORKS,
and then under H
she finds HURLY-BURLY.
What a strange word!
Kika has no idea what it means.
Maybe it's black magic?
Kika doesn't want to know
more about it. She knows
that she must be very careful
with this magic book.
OOPS, what's this?
She reads and reads
but she doesn't see and
she doesn't feel that
her hair suddenly stands on end!
It looks wild.

FIREWORKS: fuegos artificiales
her hair suddenly stands on end!: ¡su pelo se pone de punta de repente!

But Kika reads on and on.
Maybe it has something to do with
that strange word HURLY-BURLY.
Suddenly her hair turns black.
Then it turns blue,
blue like the ocean.
It's only for a moment.
Then it's over again.
"Ah, here it is," Kika says.
This is her plan:
Kika wants to help Ms Howard
so that the inspector
will give her an A+.
But Kika needs special tricks
for this plan. She finds ideas
here and there in her magic book.
She writes them all down.

reads on and on: sigue leyendo
A+: sobresaliente
here and there: de aquí y de allí

When she's done,
she closes the book very carefully
and puts it back under her bed.
Then she sits down at her desk
and looks at the piece of paper.
She giggles as she reads
her ideas again.
There are seven or eight magic spells
on the page.
She will try them out tomorrow.
And the inspector
will be very surprised . . .
There's just one little problem.
Kika can't take
the magic book to school.
First, because it's very heavy.

she's done: ha terminado
There are: Hay
will try them out: los probará
heavy: pesado

Second, because it's a secret book.
So she must learn these magic spells
over and over again.
The tricks must be perfect
for school tomorrow.
Kika knows that she can't say
these magic spells out loud.
They can be very dangerous!
So she reads
the strange words silently.
She hopes that she will learn them
like that.
But it's not easy!
After half an hour
her head is spinning...

out loud: en voz alta
silently: en voz baja
her head is spinning: su cabeza echa humo

Chapter 3

It's the next morning.
Kika can't wait to go to school!
Her plan is perfect now:
she has a piece of paper
with her magic spells
in her pocket.

In the classroom
the teacher tells the children
that the inspector will come
in the next five or ten minutes.
"Kids, please be good and please be polite,"

pocket: bolsillo
will come: vendrá

Ms Howard says again.
"And please pay attention.
Then nothing can go wrong."
The children are nervous now.
Kika is quite cool:
"Nothing will go wrong!"
She really wants to tell Ms Howard
about her plan.
She knows that
(with a little bit of magic)
everything will be fine.
But a secret witch
can't tell a single person
about her magic tricks!
One of Kika's friends, Basti, asks:
"What's he like, this inspector?"
Ms Howard answers:
"I don't know him
but the others say he . . . "

wrong: mal
cool: tranquila
little bit: un poco

There's a knock at the door.
"That's him!" All the children
turn their heads and look at the door.
Kika is the only one
who can't look at the door
because she is taking out
her little piece of paper
with the magic spells.
Then she reads the words.

One of the girls goes to the door.
Kika says some words

knock: llaman
taking out: sacando

but nobody hears her.
The door opens and . . .
Oh! It's not the inspector,
it's the school secretary, Mrs Berry.
She has some papers for Ms Howard.
"This is for you, Ms Howard,
so that you can . . . "

That is all she can say
because suddenly she trips
and lands face down on the floor.
Ms Howard runs to her.
She wants to help her to get up.
Ten children run to her.
They want to help her, too.

trips: tropieza
lands face down: se cae boca abajo

But Mrs Berry is up already
and only says:
"You're *really* polite children."
Ms Howard is still worried:
"Are you sure you're all right?"
Mrs Berry says: "Absolutely sure.
But I just don't know
how that could happen."
Well, Kika knows
how that could happen.
She doesn't say a word. She smiles.
She's happy that the trick
with the tripping
worked perfectly.
Well, not exactly perfectly
because the plan was
that the inspector should trip
and not the secretary.

how that could happen: cómo ha podido suceder
should: debería

But now they all know
that the class can be polite.
And Kika knows
that her magic trick works.
There are still many children
at the front of the classroom,
when the door opens again.
A man suddenly stands in the room.
"My name is Stuart,
Mr Michael Stuart," he shouts.
"Is this Ms Howard's class?"
"Yes, yes, I'm Ms Howard.
I'm so sorry. We have a little bit
of chaos here, as you can see."
"Oh yes, I can see that."
Then Mr Stuart goes on:
"I don't normally come in like this.
But there was nobody
in the secretary's room.

stands in: entra
shouts: grita

I asked a pupil
and he showed me to this room.
I knocked at the door
but nobody opened it and so . . ."
The secretary says:
"There's always somebody
in the secretary's room."
She knows that this man
can only be the inspector.
And she knows
that she wasn't in her room.

showed me: me trajo
can only be: solo puede ser

So she must say something
to explain the situation.
"I was only out
for two or three minutes
to bring Ms Howard some papers."
Then one boy says:
"And we normally hear
when somebody knocks at the door."
Another boy shouts: "There was just
a little bit of chaos here."
A third boy yells: "And we always
open the door, especially
for inspectors and headmasters!"
And a fourth child shouts louder
than all three together:
"Because we're
really polite children."
The inspector asks:

to explain: para explicar
yells: grita
louder: más fuerte

"Are you always like this?
Don't you ever put up your hands
when you want to say something?"
Ms Howard explains:
"The children are excited
that you're here.
This is not a normal situation.
And then Mrs Berry tripped."
Kika thinks: OUCH! This is not
what I wanted.
I must do something fast.
The inspector doesn't look very happy.
Kika takes out her piece of paper again.
But this time the spell is too strong:
WHOOPS! Half the class,
plus the inspector, the secretary,
and the teacher fall down.

Don't you ever put up your hands?: ¿Es que nunca levantáis la mano?
strong: fuerte
plus: más

Now the rest of the class
run to the others
to help them get up!
There's complete chaos now.
Kika is totally shocked.
She sits at her desk
and watches the others.
Slowly the situation goes back
to normal again.
The children go back to their desks.
Mrs Berry gets up.

shocked: perpleja
watches: mira

She says good-bye.
Then it <u>turns quiet</u> in the classroom.
Very quiet. Extremely quiet.
Ms Howard says:
"Okay . . . let's begin then."
And the inspector says:
"Never, I have never
in my <u>whole life</u> . . ."
and he writes many, many things
in his little black book.

turns quiet: se hace el silencio
whole life: toda mi vida

Ms Howard goes down
on her knees and checks
the floor.
"I just don't know.
Maybe the janitor
put too much polish on the floor.
Maybe he wanted to make
the room perfect
for you."
The inspector writes and writes.
"Never, I have never
in my whole life . . .
I must tell the school board
about this."
Kika thinks OUCH! again.
What is the inspector writing
in his little black book?

knees: rodillas
janitor: conserje
polish: cera
school board: consejo escolar

Can it be positive?
It's not the teacher's fault
when people trip by chance.
By chance . . .
Kika knows it wasn't
by chance.
The spell for tripping
is on her piece of paper, too.
Kika looks at her spells
again.
There's one spell for smoke.
It's only an emergency spell –
but is this not
an emergency now?
Kika says
some words
quietly.

trip by chance: tropiezan ellos solos
smoke: humo
emergency: emergencia

Moments later the alarm goes off.
Fire alarm!
"What's this now?"
The inspector looks at Ms Howard.
She says: "I don't think it's a fire.
It can only be a <u>fire drill</u>.
I'm sure it's only a fire drill."
The inspector looks through his book.
"Today? I don't know anything about a fire drill. Why don't they tell me about these things?"
Ms Howard says:
"Maybe it's something <u>serious</u>.
<u>You never know</u>."
The inspector doesn't think so.
"<u>Nonsense!</u>

<u>fire drill</u>: simulacro de incendio
<u>serious</u>: serio
<u>You never know</u>: Nunca se sabe
<u>Nonsense!</u>: ¡Tonterías!

I'm sure it's only a practical joke.
When I was a pupil, we always
did something . . . I mean,
we never did anything like that!"
Ms Howard isn't so sure.
"But maybe this is a real alarm now."
The inspector doesn't want to hear
more about this. "Please begin
your lesson now."
Smoke is coming into the classroom
from under the door.
All the children cry out in panic
and the inspector's face
turns white.
"Get out everybody! Get out now!"
He runs to the door.
But Ms Howard blocks the door.

practical joke: travesura
When I was a pupil: Cuando yo era estudiante
cry out in panic: gritan de pánico
blocks: bloquea

"You can't open the door," she shouts,
"that is where the smoke
is coming from!"
Mr Stuart is very nervous now:
"Then open the windows
or we will all die."
Ms Howard shakes her head.
"The windows must be closed
when there's a fire."
She goes over to the window
and stands right in front of it.
"The rules say
that you shouldn't open the windows.
If we let in fresh air,
the fire can grow bigger."
Mr Stuart says: "You're right,
you're absolutely right.

shakes her head: niega con la cabeza
fresh air: aire fresco
grow bigger: hacerse más grande

I mean I know that the windows
must be closed but I think
I was so shocked that I forgot."
His face is totally white now.
One child asks: "But what
are we going to do?"
Ms Howard is very calm:
"We must wait. But we can
do something about the smoke."

calm: calmada

She takes off her jacket, rolls it up
and puts it under the door.
The smoke can't get through now.
Other children bring their jackets.
One girl wants to take off
her pullover.
But Ms Howard doesn't let her.
"That's fine.
Please everybody sit down.
We're going to wait and see."
Suddenly Ms Howard smiles.
"Maybe this is the janitor's idea!
Maybe he's blowing cigarette smoke
through the door.
He just wants to test us
because the inspector is here.
Or maybe this is your idea,
Mr Stuart. You want to test us!"

takes off: se quita
can't get through: no puede pasar
he's blowing: él está soplando

The inspector
still doesn't look very happy.
"I can't tell you, Ms Howard.
But you're doing fine,
that's all I can say."
"Look, look, look!"
Twenty children
run to the window.
Everybody can hear it now:
a siren.
The fire brigade is here
with three vehicles.
Not long after that
somebody knocks at the door.
A fireman with a helmet
and heavy boots
tells the children to come out.

fire brigade: brigada de bomberos
vehicles: vehículos
fireman: bombero
helmet: casco
boots: botas

"Take each other by the hand
and come with me."
The rest is easy:
the children make a long line.
The inspector is at the end
(now only his nose is white).
Everybody leaves the classroom.
YUK, that smell! Kika is glad
that she's in the playground.

YUK: Ufff
glad: contenta

All the other children are glad, too.
It's good to be outside in the open.
Other classes
are in the playground, too.
Chaos at school . . .
What's the problem?
Somewhere there must be a fire.
Or is there a fire at all?

at all: en absoluto

There's smoke,
but nobody can see flames.
Can there be smoke without fire???
The firemen roll out hoses
and run back and forth.
They try to find the fire.
But after 15 minutes they give up.

flames: llamas
hoses: mangeras
back and forth: de un lado a otro
give up: se dan por vencidos

There's no fire.
Nobody has a clue.
Nobody?
Kika Superwitch has a clue.
The spell is over
but it takes some time
until the smoke is gone.
And after the smoke is gone,
the fire brigade is gone, too.
The children and the teachers
can go back to their classrooms now.

Nobody has a clue: Nadie tiene ni idea
is gone: se va

Chapter 4

The inspector is back in his chair.
(His nose is back to its normal colour.)
"Let's start, Ms Howard.
There's not much time left."
His little black book
is back on his desk.
He looks grim.
OUCH! Kika is worried.
Her idea with the emergency spell
was not very good.
What can she do now?
She looks at her piece of paper.
Ah, she has this spell for LOVE!
Kika's idea was
that the inspector should be
nice to Ms Howard but there
was no spell in her book for NICE.

There's not much time left: No nos queda mucho tiempo
grim: contrariado
should be: debería ser

Kika then remembered
what her mother always says
when she wants to be nice.
"That's lovely, dear."
Too bad that there was
nothing under DEAR and
nothing under LOVELY.
But Kika never gives up easily.
There was a spell for LOVE
in her book. That's practically
the same as nice, isn't it?
At the moment the inspector
doesn't look very nice.
And this is all Kika's fault!
It's because of Kika
that there's trouble at school!
Should she say the spell now?
It could go wrong again.

all Kika's fault: todo por culpa de Kika
trouble: lío

It's all right, Kika thinks,
the situation can't get more chaotic
than it is now.
And that's why she says
the tricky spell for LOVE.
Seconds later
the inspector looks
no longer grim.
His eyes are shining now
as he looks at the children
and at the teacher.
"Ah, Ms Howard," he smiles,
"I look at you and I must say
I'm quite fond of you."
"Sorry . . . what are you saying?"
Ms Howard doesn't have
a clue about what he is trying
to tell her.

tricky: difícil
no longer: ya no
His eyes are shining: Sus ojos están brillando
I'm quite fond of you: Me cae bastante bien

The inspector says:
"I mean, I feel so strange.
It's . . . I feel . . .
This is so funny . . .
I can't understand . . . I mean . . .
I'm not married. Are you . . .
well . . . are you married?"
Oh no! Not again!
Kika can see
that this was the wrong spell!

I feel: me siento
I mean: Quiero decir
married: casado

She says her spell once more,
this time very quickly.
She wants to <u>undo</u> the magic.
It works perfectly.
The inspector's eyes
aren't shining any more.
But Kika's class-mates
now give each other <u>hugs</u>
and kisses!
This is a big surprise
for Mr Stuart and Ms Howard.
They just sit and watch.
Kika thinks:
I must do something!
So she says her spell
for LOVE again.
She hopes that she can say
these tricky words correctly.
She sits and waits.

<u>undo</u>: deshacer
<u>hugs</u>: abrazos

Steven and Sabrina are not
normally best friends.
And now they're holding hands!
But wait, something is happening:
Sabrina gets up and shouts at Steven.
"What are you doing, you twit!
Go away and leave me alone."

best friends: buenos amigos
twit: idiota
leave me alone: déjame en paz

Kika thinks: great. Wonderful.
That's it. The spell is over.
They're all back to normal.
Not all, some are suddenly very nasty.
Peter (he sits behind Kika) gets up
and says: "This really stinks,
Ms Howard."

Wonderful: Maravilloso
nasty: groseros

All the children look at Peter.
They're shocked.
Ms Howard only says:
"Well, Peter.
You say it stinks.
I say we need some fresh air."
So she goes to the window
and opens it.
The inspector is busy
with his little black book.
He doesn't hear what is going on
in the classroom.
Now he looks up and says:
"Ms Howard, let's start
with a normal lesson. Please."
Ms Howard must do
what the inspector says.
She goes back to her desk
and looks into her bag.
She takes out five apples,
beautiful red apples.

She takes two apples in one hand
and three apples in the other hand.
Then she asks the class:
"I have two apples in my left hand
and three apples in my right hand.
What's that?"
Kika shouts as loud as she can:
"Five!"
Oh no! How could she do that!
She must always
put up her hand first!
Kika is worried
that she always does the wrong thing.
But she really
wants to help her teacher.
Ms Howard says:
"Five, that's correct. But there's
a second correct answer."
Kika doesn't have a clue.
Ms Howard wants to help her:
"It's easy, think about it!"

Lars shouts: “That’s not fair.
What Kika says is correct.
Two and three is five!”
Ms Howard says: “Correct.
But there’s a second answer.”
Lars asks: “What’s that?”
Ms Howard answers:
“You can be the teacher
and then you will see.”
Lars thinks this is great.
He goes to the teacher’s desk
and takes the apples in his hands.
He stands there like an inspector!
Then he asks the teacher:
“I have two apples in my right hand
and three apples in my left hand.
What’s that?”
Ms Howard makes a face
like a pupil that doesn’t know
the answer.

"You . . . have . . . you have . . .
five apples altogether.
Two and three
is the same as one and four.
But what I know for sure is . . ."
She makes that face again like a pupil
that must think about the answer.
The whole class is watching
and waiting.
They all want to hear the answer.
"Well, a pupil with five apples
in his two hands –
what I know for sure is
that he's very, very hungry!"
The children think this is great fun.
This is the best maths class ever.
And they think about
new questions:

altogether: en total
maths: matemáticas
ever: de todas

five and three eggs is eight.
And when they all fall down?
Then you have scrambled eggs.
Another one:
there are five flies on the window.
When you catch one, – how many do
you have on the window then?
Not a single one – they all fly away!
Kika is extremely happy.

scrambled eggs: huevos revueltos
flies: moscas
fly: vuelan

Her magic spells went all wrong,
they weren't helpful at all.
But her teacher has very good ideas
so that nothing is left
from the last spell
(when the other pupils
were very, very strange!).
Kika watches the inspector.
What's he doing?

His little black book
is still on his desk.

But he isn't writing anymore.
He puts up his hand
because he wants to say something!
Ms Howard says: "Well, Mr Stuart,
what's your question for us?"
But he has no question for the class.
He says: "Well done, Ms Howard.
It was extremely difficult
for you today
but you always know
what to do,
even in the trickiest situations."
Ms Howard is tired but she smiles.
There were so many strange things
today. She wasn't sure
what the inspector would say.
It was a good thing that she
had no idea about Kika's tricks . . .

trickiest: más complicadas
There were: Sucedieron
wasn't sure: no estaba segura
would say: diría

Then Ms Howard sends the children
to the playground.
Kika puts her piece of paper
with the magic spells
into her school bag.
Suddenly she has an idea.
She takes out
the piece of paper.
She goes out of the classroom
with the other children
and reads her spells once more.
Then she walks to the stairs
(with the others)
and says something very quietly.
She tiptoes back
to the classroom and listens
to the two people in the room.
She hears Ms Howard.

tiptoes: anda de puntillas

"But Mr Stuart," her teacher says,
"well, this really is a big surprise!"
Kika takes a quick look.
Mr Stuart is very surprised himself.
He stands there
with flowers in his hands.
He doesn't know what's happening:
"I . . . I just don't know . . . I mean . . .
why . . . suddenly . . . they were
there . . . in my hand . . ."
Ms Howard smiles:
"This is so nice of you.
They're beautiful flowers."
Mr Stuart is still very surprised.
"Yes, these flowers . . . I don't
understand . . . I mean . . .
they were suddenly in my hand . . .
in my hand . . .
and I don't know . . ."

suddenly: de repente
they were: estaban

Ms Howard takes the flowers
out of his hand and says:
"We must find a vase for them."
The inspector looks happy now
that Ms Howard has the flowers.
How *did* these flowers get there?
Kika laughs.
"One trick that works!" she says.
She runs down the hall
with her piece of paper in her hand.
She will never say magic spells again
at school . . . never! . . . never???

vase: jarrón

Index

En colaboración con la UNESCO,
KNISTER ha creado la KNISTERschool,
un proyecto solidario para construir
un colegio en la India.

Infórmate sobre este proyecto en:
http://knisterschool.knister.com/es

¡Hola!

Este que ves en la foto soy yo. Me llamo KNISTER, y soy el autor de las aventuras de Kika Superbruja.

Como siempre me ha gustado vuestro mundo, el de los chicos y chicas como tú, he escrito muchos libros y canciones para vosotros, y también obras de teatro.

Me encanta presentar programas de lectura en la tele, la radio, las bibliotecas, los teatros y las librerías de mi país (que, por cierto, es Alemania), y también disfruto mucho cuando realizo trabajos para chicos y chicas que son discapacitados psíquicos, o disléxicos, o ciegos..., todos ellos de tu misma edad.

Pero lo mejor de todo es cuando vosotros participáis conmigo en lo que hago, leyendo mis libros y compartiendo las aventuras de los personajes que los protagonizan.

En esta ocasión he querido presentaros a Kika Superbruja. Como es una bruja supersecreta, me costó bastante que me explicara sus trucos de magia, pero al final lo conseguí. Aunque..., no sé por qué, pero me da la impresión de que Kika Superbruja no me ha contado todos sus supersecretos... ¡y a lo mejor todavía le quedan unos cuantos hechizos guardados en la manga!

www.KNISTER.com

Queridos padres, queridos maestros:

La mayoría de los niños se ponen muy orgullosos cuando leen su primer libro en otro idioma (¡y con razón!), de modo que estas aventuras de Kika Superwitch en un inglés simple y pedagógicamente adaptado pueden motivar y cautivar incluso a los más principiantes.

El texto presenta un vocabulario básico de alrededor de 500 palabras, y en su desarrollo se ha tenido en cuenta la metodología de enseñanza de idiomas más actualizada.

Hasta ahora, en la enseñanza (tradicional) de idiomas se consideraba que los niños solo podían entender un texto en un idioma extranjero cuando estaban completamente familiarizados con sus estructuras gramaticales.

Sin embargo, si leen este libro, comprobarán que en él se emplean a menudo el pasado y el futuro, y también frases de relativo, todos ellos elementos que, según los planes clásicos de estudios, se tratan bastante más tarde en las aulas.

Ello se debe a que las investigaciones más recientes sobre los procesos de comprensión lectora muestran que un lector (independientemente de su edad) se concentra sobre todo en el contenido, y no en la gramática del texto.

Por ejemplo, en una frase como *"An inspector is going to come to our school tomorrow"*, realmente solo hay tres palabras relevantes: *"inspector-come-school"*, con las cuales se transmite la información decisiva para que el lector desentrañe por sí mismo su sentido, sin mayor esfuerzo.

Esto implica, tanto para la enseñanza como para la lectura en casa, que los niños pueden leer textos cuyo contenido comprendan (incluso sin conocer aún las estructuras gramaticales).

En este libro, por tanto, se emplean estas innovadoras técnicas.

Se ha procurado emplear frases lo más cortas posible, y en cuanto a las palabras de contenido importante, o son plenamente conocidas por su sencillez, o pueden deducirse por su similitud al español, o se aclaran en notas a pie de página.

Asimismo, las ilustraciones han sido cuidadosamente escogidas para narrar de forma visual las situaciones que van produciéndose en el texto.

Por último, un apunte sobre las notas de vocabulario a pie de página: Su finalidad consiste en "derribar barreras", no en erigirlas, por lo que (a diferencia de los métodos de inglés tradicionales) se han configurado de tal forma que en muchas ocasiones constan de frases o sintagmas enteros, y exigen del lector el mínimo conocimiento de gramática posible (por ejemplo, no se utilizan los infinitivos con *"to")*.

Para que sus hijos o alumnos no tengan dificultades con su primer libro de Kika en inglés, por favor, lea con ellos los consejos de lectura que figuran a continuación. Así, será imposible que algo vaya mal.

¡Que disfruten –niños y mayores– con la lectura!

Ellen Butzko y KNISTER

Trucos de lectura ultrasecretos de Kika

★ Si no entiendes lo que significa cada palabra, simplemente sigue leyendo. Te darás cuenta de que, a pesar de todo, comprendes la historia.

★ Puedes encontrar la traducción de algunas palabras difíciles en la misma página, abajo. El vocabulario traducido está subrayado en el texto.

★ Muchas palabras inglesas que aún no conoces se parecen mucho al español; por ejemplo: *"secret"*, *"ocean"*, *"problem"*, *"minute"*, *"emergency"*.

Reconocerás otras palabras porque se usan igual en español; por ejemplo: *“sheriff”*, *“revolver”*, *“comic”*, *“idea”*, *“super”*.

Una cosa genial:
¡En este libro aprenderás palabras que seguro que tu profe de inglés no te enseña! Por ejemplo:
“fart” (=tirarse un pedo),
“twit” (=idiota).

Últimos títulos de la colección «Kika Superbruja»

0. *Kika Superbruja y el libro de hechizos*

16. *Kika Superbruja y los dinosaurios*

17. *Kika Superbruja y sus bromas mágicas*

18. *Kika Superbruja y la aventura espacial*

19. *Kika Superbruja en el país de Liliput*

20. *Kika Superbruja y el examen del dragón*

21. *Kika Superbruja y el viaje a Mandolán*

22. *Kika Superbruja y el reino mágico*

Nueva colección «Kika Superbruja» EN COLOR Y CON OLOR

Kika Superbruja revoluciona la clase

Kika Superbruja y los piratas

Kika Superbruja y la magia del circo

Kika Superbruja y sus bromas mágicas

Kika Superbruja, detective

Kika Superbruja en el Salvaje Oeste

Kika Superbruja, loca por el fútbol

Kika Superbruja y los indios

Últimos títulos de la colección «Kika Superbruja y Dani»

11. *Un fantasma en el colegio*
12. *El misterioso genio de la botella*
13. *Un delfín en el jardín*

Cuaderno para colorear

Kika Superbruja y Dani y sus fantásticas aventuras

Kika Superbruja y Dani y sus historias mágicas

Especiales Kika Superbruja

Especial cumpleaños - Especial Navidad

Libro de magia - El mundo de Kika

Superpasatiempos

Kika Superbruja y el libro de hechizos
(EDICIÓN ESPECIAL N.º 0 CON FOTOS DE LA PELÍCULA)

Kika Superbruja y el libro de hechizos
(ÁLBUM DE LA PELÍCULA)

Kika Superbruja y el viaje a Mandolán
(EDICIÓN ESPECIAL N.º 21 CON FOTOS DE LA PELÍCULA)

Kika Superbruja y el viaje a Mandolán
(ÁLBUM DE LA PELÍCULA)

Colección «Todo sobre...»

1. *Todo sobre los piratas*
2. *Todo sobre los dinosaurios*
3. *Todo sobre los antiguos egipcios*
4. *Todo sobre los caballeros*
5. *Todo sobre los delfines y las ballenas*
6. *Todo sobre los caballos*

Colección «Kika Superwitch»

1. *Kika Superwitch Trouble at School*
2. *Kika Superwitch at Vampire Castle*

Colección «Kika Superwitch & Dani»

1. *Kika Superwitch & Dani Magic Homework*
2. *Kika Superwitch & Dani And the Wild Dinosaurs*
3. *Kika Superwitch & Dani And the Birthday Party*

Colección «Vacaciones con Kika»

(6 CUADERNOS PARA EDUCACIÓN PRIMARIA)

Colección «Holidays with Kika Superwitch»

(6 CUADERNOS PARA EDUCACIÓN PRIMARIA)

Si te gustan los libros de Kika, ¡no te pierdas estos otros del mismo autor!

Colección «Yoko»

1. *¿Quién diablos es Yoko?*
2. *Yoko alborota la escuela*
3. *Yoko y la noche del terror*

Colección «Quique & Lucas, locopilotos»

1. *La sorpresa del abuelo*
2. *3, 2, 1… ¡despegando!*
3. *Misión secreta*
4. *A la conquista del espacio*

Colección «Altamar»

140. *Willy, la mosca*
149. *El huevo prehistórico*

Colección «Álbumes ilustrados»

Te lo prometo
El gran baile de Sofía y su abuela
La bella Beba

ARABESK